WONDERFUL WORLD OF KNOWLEDGE

Stories

Wonderful World of Knowledge

GROLIER ENTERPRISES, INC.
Danbury, Connecticut

ROBERT B. CLARKE   *Publisher*

ARNOLDO MONDADORI EDITORE

MARIO GENTILINI	*Editor-in-Chief*
ELISA PENNA	*Supervising Editor*
GIOVAN BATTISTA CARPI CLAUDIO MAZZOLI	*Illustrators*
ELISA PENNA	*Author*

ISBN 0-7172-8164-7
"Disney's WONDERFUL WORLD OF KNOWLEDGE"
is an updated and enlarged English version of
an encyclopedia heretofore printed in the Italian language by
ARNOLDO MONDADORI EDITORE, MILAN
and entitled (in English Translation) "Disney ENCYCLOPEDIA"

100

CONTENTS

The Adventures of Gilgamesh 9

The Lion and the Mouse 15

The Crow and the Jug 16

The Mosquito and the Bull 17

Ali Baba and the Forty Thieves 19

Aladdin and His
Wonderful Lamp 24

The Genie of the River 29

The Peasant and His Sons 33

The Wolf and the Stork 34

The Banker and the Cobbler 35

Tom Thumb 37

Blue Beard 41

Princess Briar Rose 43

Hansel and Gretel 45

The Seven Ravens 49

Rapunzel 51

The Magic Table 54

The Bremen Town Musicians 57

The King of the Golden Mountain 60

The Shoemaker and the Elves 61

The Little Mermaid 65

The Red Shoes 68

The Emperor's New Clothes 70

The Little Match Girl 73

The Eleven Wild Swans 76

The Princess and the Pea 79

The Little Tin Soldier 82

The Tinder Box 84

The Song of Hiawatha 86

The Sleeping Beauty 91

Snow White and the
Seven Dwarfs 99

Cinderella 109

The Ugly Duckling 116

Puss In Boots 118

Little Red Riding Hood 121

Index 124

Welcome, children! Welcome to the wonderful world of make believe. We're about to set out on an exciting journey to a land of genies and goblins, fairies and elves, where pots of gold lie at the end of the rainbow, and princes and princesses live happily ever after.

Now, for the benefit of those of you who don't know me, I'd like to introduce myself. My name is Snow White, and these are my friends the Seven Dwarfs. All of us—Sneezy, Doc, Dopey, Bashful, Happy, Grumpy, Sleepy, and I—live in story land, and we know it very well. That's why we're going to be your guides on our enchanted journey.

Your're going to hear some of the world's most wonderful tales. In some of them, called fables, you'll meet talking animals who might possibly teach you a lesson. These well known stories were told by Aesop, Phaedrus, and La Fontaine, some of the world's greatest fabulists.

In fairy tales you'll meet magicians and witches and fearless knights. Magic carpets will carry you to kingdoms you never heard of, and genies will grant your smallest wish. Hans Christian Andersen, the brothers Grimm, and Charles Perrault have written down some of our best-loved fairy tales. You'll also read exciting stories about the brave deeds of legendary heroes.

We're going to begin our great adventure with a story about an ancient Babylonian hero named Gilgamesh, a tale that was told thousands of years ago, in a time so distant that there was neither paper nor ink. But people loved the story, and generation after generation, parents told their children tales of the adventures of Gilgamesh, and the legends lived.

So take my hand, children, we're on our way. Follow the dwarfs and me as we lead you into the magic land of make-believe!

THE ADVENTURES OF GILGAMESH

Once upon a time in the ancient city of Uruk there lived a brave young king named Gilgamesh. When Gilgamesh was born, the gods bestowed upon him the gifts of courage and ambition. As Gilgamesh grew to manhood, these qualities made him restless and dissatisfied with his kingdom and all the wonderful things he possessed.

The people of Uruk began to complain about their young king, and the

9

gods decided to teach Gilgamesh a lesson. Keeping their plan a secret, they created a good and kindly man named Enkidú, who was a friend of the beasts of the fields and forests. The hunters of Uruk soon found that they were no longer able to snare wild animals, and the traps they set always remained empty. Finally they realized that it was Enkidú who was responsible, and a delegation of citizens decided to seek the help of the king.

When Gilgamesh heard of the plight of the hunters, he ordered that Enkidú be put to death. But when Enkidú was brought before him, the king was so taken by the young man's pleasant ways that the two became fast friends.

One day, much to the king's despair, Enkidú fell ill. For 9 days and 9 nights Gilgamesh himself tended and nursed his beloved friend. Finally, on the 9th night, Enkidú died in his arms. Now Gilgamesh realized that the gods had not given him the gift of immortality, and that one day he too must die. So he set out on a long journey to find his ancient ancestor Ut-napishtim, who was said to have the secret of eternal life. One day Gilgamesh came to a mountain so high that its peak was hidden in the clouds. He decided to climb the steep slopes.

When he reached the very top of the mountain, Gilgamesh was dazzled by what he saw, for he stood before the magnificent Gate of the Sun. Slowly he crossed the threshold and found himself in an unknown world surrounded by strange and beautiful creatures he had never seen before.

When Gilgamesh saw that the strange creatures were friendly, he lost no time in seeking their help. At first all of them refused to tell him how to find his ancient ancestor Ut-napishtim. But finally a lovely nymph named Siduri took pity on him and agreed to lead him to the old man's cave.

Overjoyed at arriving at the end of his

10

Weary from his labors, the happy Gilgamesh lay down on the shore to rest before embarking on his homeward journey. Placing the magic plant carefully beside him, he fell into a deep sleep. While he slept, a serpent slithered close to him. Without disturbing the sleeping king, the serpent snatched the plant of immortality, and immediately devoured it. When Gilgamesh awoke he searched far and wide for the precious plant, but he was never to find it again.

And so it was that Gilgamesh lived out his days, and died. Some people say that snakes seem to become young again when they shed their skins in the spring because of the serpent who, thousands of years ago, tasted the plant of immortality.

search at last, Gilgamesh began at once to seek Ut-napishtim's advice.

"Ancient father," he said, "I have traveled many miles and had many strange adventures, and now at last I am before you. Tell me, I beseech you, the secret of your endless days."

But Ut-napishtim slowly shook his head. And the more Gilgamesh begged and pleaded, the more the old man refused to speak.

Gilgamesh finally abandoned all hope. He was about to embark on the long journey back to his kingdom when Ut-napishtim's wife took pity on him and decided to answer his plea.

"What all men seek, O King," she whispered, "lies at the bottom of a distant sea. It is the plant of eternal life, and he who eats of it will be granted immortality."

Gilgamesh thanked the old woman and eagerly set out once more. Knowing that victory would soon be his, he made his way quickly to the sea, dove deep into its depths, and plucked the precious plant.

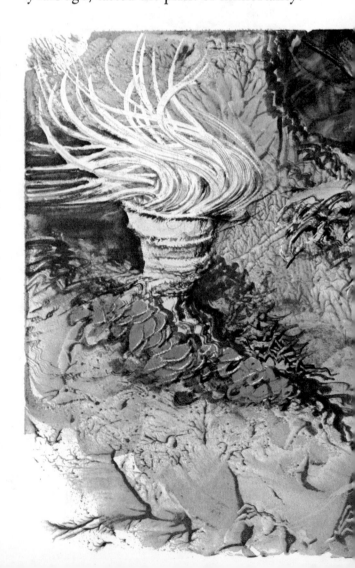

12

THE LION AND
THE MOUSE

Once upon a time there lived a tiny mouse who was very absentminded. He always forgot what he was about to do and never paid any attention to where he was going.

One day as he was scampering about he stumbled against the paws of a huge sleeping lion. Quick as a wink the lion awoke and trembling with anger, grasped the poor little mouse in his paws.

"Ah ha!" he roared. "So this is how you show respect for the king of the beasts!"

The little mouse squeaked helplessly. "Please don't eat me," he begged. "It is true that you could swallow all of me in one bite. But set me free, and perhaps some day I will be able to return the favor."

So comical was the idea that a tiny mouse might ever be able to do a favor for a huge lion that the king of the beasts burst into peals of laughter. And just because he was so amused, he opened his paws and let his little prisoner escape.

Some days later the mouse was running helter-skelter through the fields once more. Suddenly an angry roar attracted his attention. He looked around and saw

15

the lion hopelessly trapped in a hunter's net.

"Oh, Your Majesty," cried the mouse, "what has happened to you?"

"Can't you see for yourself?" roared the lion. "I'm trapped in a net, and I can't possibly get myself free."

Suddenly the mouse had an idea. He scampered straight to the net and, quick as a wink, began to gnaw on the ropes. In less time than it takes to tell, he had set the lion free.

The moral of this fable is: It's always better to be kind to everyone.

THE CROW AND THE JUG

One hot day a crow, so thirsty his throat seemed to be on fire, was flying round and round in search of water. The poor crow was about to drop from weariness when he spied, in the middle of a stone quarry, a large jug.

Hardly daring to hope, he swooped down. At the bottom of the jug was some water.

Swooping down, the mosquito landed on top of the bull's left horn. She cleared her throat slightly and said:

"I hope I'm not too heavy for you, sir. If I am, I beg you to say so truthfully and you can be sure I'll be on my way."

"As you like, little girl!" answered the bull. "But the truth is, I didn't even realize you'd landed, so I certainly won't notice when you go."

Now, children, Doc wants to tell you what this fable means.

"The storal of the morey," says Doc, "or rather, the moral of the story is this: Sometimes those who think they are the most important are really the most insignificant."

The thirsty crow lighted on the rim and stretched his neck as far as he could into the jug's mouth. But try as he might, he could not make his beak reach the water. He was about to give up in despair when he remembered that he was in a quarry.

The crafty crow hit on a bright idea. He picked up a stone, carried it to the jug, and dropped it in. Then he took a second stone and a third, until gradually the level of the water was high enough for him to reach.

So the crow learned something many of us already know: Sometimes impossible situations work out fine if we use our heads.

THE MOSQUITO
AND THE BULL

A mosquito, feeling rather tired after a long flight, decided to stop and rest. She was a very conceited mosquito, and very fussy about where she rested. Searching for a suitable place, she spied a bull in a nearby field.

ALI BABA AND
THE FORTY THIEVES

In a little town in ancient Persia there once lived two brothers, Kassim and Ali Baba. When their father died, he left a small field to Kassim, who then married a very rich woman. Ali Baba, who had been left nothing in his father's will, owned only three donkeys, who helped him gather firewood. Nevertheless, he chose to marry the girl of his dreams, who was just as poor as he was.

One day Ali Baba said good-bye to his wife and set off as usual to search the countryside for firewood. As he was loading the wood on the donkeys' backs, he was startled by the sound of galloping horses. Alarmed, he hid his donkeys and climbed to a high branch of a nearby tree.

And just in time! From his perch Ali watched as forty fierce-looking horsemen, armed to the teeth, passed beneath the tree and stopped near a huge rock. They dismounted, and the biggest and ugliest of the horsemen stood in front of the rock, raised his sword, and commanded "Open Sesame!"

Wonder of wonders! No sooner had 19

the words been uttered than the rock trembled and opened. The horsemen disappeared through the opening, and the cave door closed behind them. After several minutes the door opened once more, and the bandits reappeared and mounted their horses. The leader raised his sword again, uttered the words "Close Sesame!"

and the rocks came together. Then the forty horsemen galloped away.

Before the dust had cleared, the astonished Ali scampered down from the tree and stood before the rock. In a voice shaking with excitement he commanded "Open Sesame!"

No sooner were the words out of his

mouth than the rocks sprang open. Before Ali's eyes were rows of shelves piled high with chests overflowing with precious jewels and gold and silver coins.

At once Ali Baba ran for his donkeys. He removed the firewood from their backs, and replaced it with six chests of coins. Then he uttered the command "Close Sesame!" The door of the cave sprang shut, and Ali returned home as swiftly as he could.

Ali Baba's wife could hardly control her excitement. Wishing to weigh the gold her husband had brought, she rushed to the house of Kassim to borrow a scale. But her sister-in-law, curious to know why the scale was needed, spread it with a layer of fat. When the scale was returned, one of the gold coins was stuck to its surface. Wild with jealousy, she immediately sent Kassim to investigate, and Ali Baba was forced to tell the truth.

Kassim could hardly wait to try his luck. The very next morning he took ten mules and went to the cave. He stood in front of the rocks and cried "Open Sesame!" Again the rocks parted, and

Kassim began to load the mules with treasures.

But alas for Kassim! Just as he was about to leave for home, the thieves appeared. Furious because their secret had been discovered, they cut off Kassim's head and threw his body into the cave.

When Kassim failed to return home, Ali Baba set out to look for him. He searched and searched, but Kassim was nowhere to be found. Finally Ali went to the cave and said the magic words. Sure enough, when the door opened, there lay Kassim's body. Ali wrapped it in a cape and took it home.

Not long afterward the thieves returned to the cave. When they discovered that Kassim's body had been removed, they realized that someone else knew of their hiding place. Their captain vowed to seek the stranger out and kill him.

But the leader of the thieves, shrewd and crafty though he was, was no match for his enemy. Ali Baba had by this time acquired a slave girl named Morgiana, a beautiful and quick-witted maiden who was completely loyal to her master. Ali Baba revealed all his secrets to her and the two of them managed to outwit the thieves.

Finally the infuriated captain hit upon a plan. He hid each of his thieves in a large jar, loaded all the jars onto mules, and set off for Ali Baba's house disguised as a rich traveler.

"Now," he thought as he rode along, "I will be able to catch this Ali Baba. I and my band will enter his house, and when the moment is right we will attack."

The captain and his heavily laden mules soon presented themselves at the gates of Ali Baba's house, where the bandit asked for food and lodging. Ali Baba ordered a great feast to be prepared, and he sat down to eat and drink with the stranger. But the wily Morgiana recognized the captain immediately, and began to figure out a way to thwart his plan.

When night fell the bandit was about to order his men out of the jugs. But Morgiana, recognizing the danger her master was in, poured a pitcher of boiling oil into each of the jugs. Then she drew from the folds of her long robe a dagger, which she thrust into the heart of the bandit, killing him with one blow.

Ali Baba was stunned, but Morgiana lost no time in explaining. "I did it for you, my master," she said. "This man was

23

the leader of the thieves, who now lie dead in those jugs."

Ali Baba, recovering from his surprise, was overwhelmed at the service the brave girl had performed. In order to repay her for her courage, he gave her to his son in marriage. And the two young people, who had loved each other for a long time, lived happily ever after.

ALADDIN AND HIS WONDERFUL LAMP

Many years ago, far, far away in a village in ancient China, lived a beggar boy named Aladdin. One day while Aladdin was roaming the streets, a mysterious magician, disguised as the boy's long-lost uncle, suddenly appeared before him. He persuaded Aladdin to leave the village and accompany him on a journey.

In the course of their travels, the magician stopped in a deserted place. There he lit a fire, threw some incense into the flames, and uttered some magic words. Suddenly a deep black hole appeared. Then the magician reached into the pocket of his cloak and withdrew a ring.

"Take this ring," he said to Aladdin, "and go down into the hole. There you will find an old lamp. If you have any trouble, just rub the ring, and a genie will appear to help you."

Aladdin did as he was told, and soon found the lamp. But the magician refused to help him out of the hole until the lamp was safe in his own hands, and Aladdin, for his part, refused to give up the lamp until he was safely on the ground. Finally the angry magician picked up a handful of dust and, uttering some magic words, threw it down the hole onto Aladdin. In no time at all the boy found himself deep within the depths of the earth, doomed to die of hunger and thirst.

Suddenly Aladdin remembered the magic ring. Hardly daring to believe in its power, he rubbed the stone and ordered the genie to appear. No sooner said than done! The genie whisked the boy and the magic lamp out of the depths and far away from the wicked magician. And soon, thanks to the genies of the lamp and the ring, Aladdin became the richest lad in the world.

One day a messenger came through the streets. He was the messenger of the Sultan, who governed the country, and he announced to one and all that Moon Flower, the beautiful daughter of the Sultan, would be given in marriage to the handsomest and richest young man in the kingdom.

Without thinking twice, Aladdin set out for the palace. But when he arrived, he was thrown into prison, for how could a common citizen dare to hope to marry a princess of royal blood? But Moon Flower, who had caught a glimpse of

Aladdin and fallen hopelessly in love with him, begged her father to free him.

The Sultan decided to go to the prison. When news of his visit reached Aladdin, he rubbed his lamp and ordered the genie to bring forth one thousand slaves bearing basins filled with precious jewels.

When the Sultan saw all these riches, he was so excited that he ordered the prisoner released.

Aladdin and Moon Flower were married in an elaborate ceremony. Aladdin never revealed to his bride the source of his wealth, and Moon Flower paid no attention to the dusty old lamp that lay in the corner of the bedroom.

One day as Moon Flower sat alone in her room, she heard a voice coming from the street.

"Any lamps for sale?" it called out. "Old lamps, used lamps—I'll trade them for new lamps and pay money for them besides."

Moon Flower, not recognizing the magician, decided that this would be a splendid opportunity to get rid of Aladdin's broken old lamp. So she rushed to the window and threw the precious possession down into the street.

Imagine the magician's joy when he held in his hand the magic lamp! And imagine, too, his happiness when he caught a glimpse of the beautiful princess. The minute he saw her he fell hopelessly in love. He was determined to marry her and, mustering all his powers, he arranged to kidnap her.

Alas poor Aladdin! Both of his most cherished possessions were lost to him. Then he remembered his ring and, rubbing its stone, he summoned the ring genie.

"Take me to Moon Flower," he ordered. And in less time than it takes to tell, he found himself in the magician's palace.

"There is not a second to waste," he said to Moon Flower. "Here is a magic potion. When the magician comes in, tell him you will become his bride, and offer a toast to the marriage."

Aladdin had barely enough time to hide behind a curtain when the wicked magician entered Moon Flower's room.

"Well, what have you decided?" he asked.

"To become your wife," answered Moon Flower sweetly. "Should we not drink to the happy event?"

The joyful magician eagerly drank the potion, and immediately fell into a sound sleep. Then Aladdin came out of his hiding place. He found his lamp, and ordered the genie to set everything right once more. And in no time at all, he and Moon Flower were back in the palace, where they lived happily ever after.

28

THE GENIE OF
THE RIVER

One day Ghiase, a young, noble warrior of a far-off African village, was out hunting leopard with some of his companions. Suddenly, in a clearing in the woods, he spied a beautiful maiden from another village. So lovely was she that Ghiase immediately fell in love with her. He returned to his own village to ask his parents if he might marry her. Finally his father said:

"According to the custom of our tribe, you should marry a girl from your own village. But if this maiden is as good and beautiful as you say, she will no doubt be loved by our people. Go, then, Ghiase, and arrange to have Sambu brought here as your bride."

Ghiase, his heart filled with happiness, sent two of his trusted men to arrange the wedding date with the girl's parents, who promised that very shortly they would send Sambu to Ghiase's village.

Soon everyone in Sambu's village was busy with the wedding preparations. And 29 some days later Sambu went off to her new village accompanied by her sister and a handmaiden.

But along the way the slave began to envy her mistress' good fortune, and a plan took shape in her mind. She invited Sambu to bathe in a river that she knew was enchanted. As soon as Sambu put her foot in the water, the River Genie appeared. In the wink of an eye, he grabbed the girl and dragged her down to the bottom of the river.

The little sister cried in vain. The slave girl threatened her harshly and ordered her not to say a word of what happened. Then the slave disguised herself as Sambu, and the two took off for Ghiase's village.

You can imagine how disappointed everyone was when they saw that the bride seemed neither good nor beautiful. Ghiase was more surprised than anyone, and he began to find excuses to postpone the wedding.

One day the little sister sat at the

river's edge, crying at her cruel fate, when suddenly Sambu appeared in the waves.

"Take heart, little one!" she said. "Someday all our sufferings will end. I have heard your cries, and the Genie, who is good to me, has let me come to you. But if you don't wish to lose me forever, you must not tell a soul, not even Ghiase, that I am here. For if you do, the Genie will never let me leave the river's depths again."

Feeling much consoled, the little girl returned to the false Sambu. The slave girl, angered that the child was no longer sad, began to scold her. To flee the slave's wrath, the little one ran to the riverbank. Not knowing that one of Ghiase's warriors was hidden neary, she called again to Sambu.

When the faithful warrior saw what happened, he ran at once to tell Ghiase and Ghiase's parents. Ghiase and his family decided to ask the River Witch if there was some way to save Sambu.

After a long time, the River Witch said: "We must find a way to make the slave girl follow Sambu's sister to the riverbank. Then I will work my magic."

Then the River Witch went to the river, and before very long Sambu reappeared. The witch quickly grasped her hand and pulled her to the shore. Ghiase was speechless with joy, for he immediately recognized his true bride.

In the meantime, Sambu's sister was trying to lure the wicked slave girl to the river's edge. She cried and cried, and threatened to give away the handmaiden's secret. But the slave, angry though she was, refused to leave her room and chase the little girl.

Finally the little girl turned to the wicked slave and cried: "Of all the women on the face of the earth, you are the

most evil. It was you who had my sister spirited away, you who have made me keep silence. But the end of your wickedness is near!"

"How dare you speak that way to me!" hissed the slave girl, raising her hand to strike. But Sambu's sister was too quick for her. Turning on her heels, she began to race toward the river, and this time the slave followed.

They ran and ran, and finally the river came into view. There on the banks stood Sambu in all her loveliness, with the happy Ghiase at her side.

When the slave girl saw them she became so terrified that she began to run wildly, helter-skelter, until finally she stepped too close to the water's edge. At that moment the River Genie appeared, and grasping the slave's hand, he pulled her into the deep behind him.

Soon Ghiase and Sambu were wed, as had been planned long ago. The wicked slave girl has never been seen again.

The 17th-century Frenchman, Jean de la Fontaine, wrote some of the world's best-loved fables.

THE PEASANT AND HIS SONS

There once was a peasant who had three sons. The peasant was a hardworking man who labored in the fields from morning until night. As a result, his harvests were large. After a lifetime of hard work the peasant became a rich man.

But the three sons, unlike their father, were lazy and greedy. They refused to help in the fields, and all they cared about was squandering their father's money.

One day the father became ill. He soon realized that he was going to die and, worried about what would happen to his lazy sons, he summoned them to his bedside.

"My sons," began the peasant. "I am an old man. In a short time I will no longer be here to provide the money you require. But far beneath the ground of this farm that you will inherit lies a great treasure. If you dig the earth, and hoe and shovel it inch by inch, you will find the treasure, I'm sure." And having said this, the old peasant died.

The three sons could hardly wait to begin searching for the treasure their father had spoken of. With shovels, picks, and hoes they started looking for the promised riches. They worked from early morning until night, and turned up the earth in every corner of the farm. But though they dug as hard as they could and left no clod of earth unturned, 33

they could find no trace of what they were looking for.

And of course it happened that the fields, which had been dug and plowed with such great care and diligence, produced an excellent harvest. In fact the harvest was so abundant that the sons had no place to store it. So they took it to market, and when people saw the lovely vegetables and fruits, they were willing to pay very high prices for them. So the sons found themselves even richer than their father was.

At last they understood how wise their father had been, for he had indeed left them a precious treasure. Now they agreed that work was worth far more than money. From then on there were no better workers than the wise peasant's three sons.

THE WOLF AND THE STORK

Once upon a time there was a wolf who had an enormous appetite. He never seemed able to satisfy his hunger and gulped everything down with great speed. One day as he was gobbling a delicious

meal, a large bone became lodged in his throat. It soon became clear that he would surely choke to death.

Just as the poor wolf was about to give up hope, a stork who was flying overhead heard his cries. Luckily the bird had studied medicine, and so he decided to see if he could be of service. After a careful examination, the stork offered to perform an operation to remove the bone.

"How much will you pay me if I am successful?" he asked.

"I'll give you the most priceless gift on earth, one that has no equal," mumbled the wolf, who could barely speak.

The stork immediately set to work. Telling the wolf to open his mouth as wide as possible, the bird thrust its beak, head, and neck into the beast's mouth and removed the bone in a jiffy.

The wolf was overjoyed. Now he could swallow once again. He was about to set out in search of a tasty meal when the stork said: "See here, my friend, you promised to pay me. Now that you're cured, I'd like to collect my fee."

The clever wolf had a ready answer. "But surely you can understand that I've already paid you. Indeed, I have given you the most precious gift in the world. For I held your head in my throat and your neck between my teeth. I could have devoured you with one swift bite, and yet I did not. So go now, and consider yourself fortunate."

And go the stork did, feeling foolish and cheated. He promised himself that in the future he would request payment in advance.

THE BANKER AND THE COBBLER

Once upon a time there lived a cobbler and a banker. The first was as poor as the second was rich. Their natures were also opposite, for the cobbler was a happy man, whereas the banker was not. What annoyed the banker most of all was that at night he tossed and turned, while the cobbler slept peacefully and always awoke rested and full of energy.

One day the banker could stand it no longer. He decided to find out why the cobbler was such a happy man. So he summoned the cobbler to his house.

"How much do you earn a year?" asked the banker, who believed that happiness could be measured only in terms of wealth.

"Oh, Your Excellency," answered the cobbler, "I don't count too well, nor do I really care. I live each day as it comes and never worry about the next."

"Well, then, just tell me how much you earn in one day," insisted the rich man.

"How much do I earn, Excellency? I earn what I need. And even that would be too much were it not for all the Sundays and holidays when I must close my shop."

The banker liked the cobbler. He wished to thank him for coming to his house, so he presented the poor man with a bag of 100 gold coins.

To the cobbler these coins, which meant so little to the banker, seemed a great fortune. He decided to hide the bag, so that he would have the money if ever he should need it. When he returned to his small house on the outskirts of the town, he dug a big hole in a secluded corner of the garden, threw the bag into it, and covered it with dirt.

"Now," he thought, "I will never be in want, and will always have more money than I need."

But from that day on the cobbler's life was changed. He began to worry about the safety of his money. Every night he slept a little less, and every time he heard the slightest sound, he was certain that thieves were stealing his coins.

Finally he could bear his unhappiness no longer. He went to the garden, dug up the coins, and returned them to the banker.

"Take back your coins," he said, "and I will be peaceful once again."

The cobbler had learned an important lesson, and so had the banker.

*Charles Perrault (1628–1703) is best known for
collections of fairy tales in prose and verse.*

TOM THUMB

Far, far away, where the earth meets
the kingdom of fairies and wizards, lay
a hut in the midst of a great forest. In
the hut lived a husband and wife, two
good people getting on in years. They
were quite happy and had little to complain about, and their only sorrow was
that they had not been blessed with children.

One day, as they sat talking about how
nice it would be to have a little one to
gladden their home, they heard a knock
on the door. The wife answered the
knock and welcomed the unexpected
guest kindly. She offered him a place at
the table and some dinner. The guest was
pleased by this hospitality, and when he
had finished dining he said:

"You have both been so kind to me
that I should like to make you a gift. My
name is Merlin. I am a magician, and I
have great power. So tell me what it is
you would like to have."

Then the wife, hardly daring to hope,
decided to ask for the one thing they
lacked.

"I'm sure it would not be possible,"
she began, "but what we'd really like to
have, more than anything in the world,
is a little child."

"A child?" asked Merlin.

"Even a very tiny child, as small as   37

my husband's thumb," replied the old woman.

"Agreed!" said Merlin, and disappeared.

The following morning, when the husband and wife awoke, they could hardly believe their eyes. There on the doorstep was a little child, just as Merlin had promised. The baby was so tiny, so very, very tiny, that they had to squint to see him. They were afraid they might not be able to take care of him, so they went to ask the advice of the fairies who lived nearby. Nemorina, the leader of the fairies, said:

"Since the child is so small, I think we should name him Tom Thumb." And that's how the little boy got his name.

Though Tom grew older he never became any taller than his father's thumb. His parents loved him and the fairies protected him. Nemorina made him a present of a dangerous weapon—a tiny sword, no larger than a common pin.

Now Tom was a good boy, but he was very curious, and his curiosity was always getting him into trouble. One day as his mother was baking a cake, he climbed up the side of the mixing bowl to see what she was stirring. And just when she looked away for a minute, Tom lost his balance and slid right down into the batter with a splash. His mother, noticing a tiny lump in the bowl, thought a fly had fallen into it, and before Tom could protest, she opened the kitchen window and threw out all the batter.

It happened that a river ran right underneath that very window, so poor Tom Thumb wound up in the water. At that very moment a fish went swimming by, with its mouth wide open. And of course Tom was swept into the fish's mouth. One big swallow, and Tom was down in the dark depths of the fish's stomach.

And it also happened that on that day the king's cook decided to go fishing for a fine fish for the king's dinner. The cook was delighted with the splendid fish he caught, and took it back to the palace kitchen to prepare it. When he cut the fish open, who should come sliding out

of its belly but Tom! And poor Tom raised such a howl that the noise reached the royal ears of the king.

"Great snakes and dragons!" roared the king as he stormed into the kitchen. "What is the meaning of all this racket?" When he heard what had happened he was so amused that he ordered Tom to stay in the palace and live at his side.

The two spent all their time together, and Tom began to enjoy his new life enormously. Since the king was a great hunter, he provided Tom with a fiery steed—a tiny mouse with a fine saddle and bridle—so that he could join the hunt.

One day as the two were hunting in the forest, a huge cat appeared. The cat, an enormous animal with flashing eyes, spied Tom's mount and immediately attacked the little mouse.

Quick as a flash, Tom drew his magic sword and prepared for battle. He fought a long, hard, furious fight to save his own life and that of his faithful steed. Finally his sword struck the cat a fatal blow, and the battle was over.

Little by little Tom began to weary of his life at court. More and more often his thoughts turned to his dear parents and their humble hut in the forest, and he realized that he missed them very much indeed.

Tom asked the king for permission to return home. But His Majesty liked having the tiny boy around, and refused to permit him to leave. Tom became sadder and sadder, and longed for his home more and more.

Finally Nemorina, the leader of the fairies, took pity on Tom. She decided that he had at last learned his lesson, and would never again be so curious. So, with her band of faithful fairies, she managed to set the little boy free, and in no time at all he was back at home with his parents once more.

BLUE BEARD

Once upon a time there was a mighty lord named Blue Beard. He lived in a great castle on a hill. Every mother in the village wanted her daughter to marry this rich and powerful lord. Blue Beard, for his part, wanted his bride to be the most obedient maiden in the country. He issued a decree saying that those who wished him for a husband would stay in the castle as his guests while he judged them.

One day the poor widowed mother of three good and beautiful daughters decided to send her oldest daughter to Blue Beard. But, alas, the poor girl was never seen again, and Blue Beard explained that she had gone off to marry a handsome knight.

Some time later the widow sent her second daughter to Blue Beard, and this girl met the same fate as her sister. Now only one daughter remained at home, the beautiful and kind Rose Red.

One day Rose Red said to her mother: "Please, Mother, let me go to Blue Beard's castle. I will try to pass the test and, at the same time, see if I can learn something of my sisters' fate."

At first the widow refused to let Rose Red leave her side, but the girl begged and pleaded until her mother consented.

Blue Beard welcomed the girl graciously. He showed her his vast estate and finally led her to the castle. Rose Red was enchanted, for she had never seen such riches. Then Blue Beard said:

"Rose Red, you are a good and beautiful girl, but I must make sure that you are obedient as well, so I will put you to the test. You see before you thirteen rooms. Twelve of them you may enter freely. But the thirteenth belongs only to me, and you must never go into it."

Rose Red agreed, and the two passed several happy days together. One day Blue Beard announced that he had business in a distant town and would have to be away from the castle for a while. Before he left, he cautioned Rose Red once more against opening the door of the thirteenth room.

No sooner had Blue Beard left than Rose Red, overcome with curiosity, went to the corridor with the thirteen doors. She tiptoed to the forbidden room and quietly pushed open the heavy door. And there, much to her surprise, she found her sisters and many other girls from the village, dressed in rags and living in misery. Quickly Rose Red began to free the poor girls. But just at that moment Blue Beard returned from his journey. He flew into a furious rage and was about to take out his anger on Rose Red, when the girl threw herself down at his feet and pleaded:

"Forgive me, my lord, for I have disobeyed you. But before you decide the punishment that shall be mine, listen to my story. In truth, I did not come here to marry you. I came instead to discover the fate of these girls. I care little about your riches, and all I ask of the man I marry is love. But I have lived here with you for some time and I have learned to love you and to understand many things. All I ask is that you release these girls and allow them to return home. And in exchange for their freedom I offer you my life."

At first Blue Beard's rage was so great that he could barely listen to the girl's plea. But he had grown to love her dearly, and as she spoke his anger gradually passed. So he released the girls and gave his castle and all its riches to the poor of the village. Then he and Rose Red were married, and they lived happily ever after in a simple cottage at the edge of a wood.

PRINCESS BRIAR ROSE

Once upon a time a king decided to give his only daughter, the beautiful Princess Briar Rose, in marriage to the elderly ruler of the neighboring kingdom. Princess Briar Rose tried as hard as she could to put off the wedding day. She asked her father to have three gowns made for her: one made from the rays of the sun, the second from the light of the moon, and the third from the blue velvet of a starry night. She thought that this would be so difficult that she would never have to marry the old king.

But the king managed somehow to have the three gowns made for his daughter. They arrived packed in a golden nutshell. Then the king insisted that she get ready for her marriage. In desperation, Princess Briar Rose fled the castle.

She wandered far and wide, walking by day and sleeping in trees at night, until she began to resemble a wild creature. One day she was discovered by a prince. "Who are you?," he asked. "My lord, have pity on me," begged the girl. "All I ask is a place to sleep and a morsel of food, for I have nowhere to go." Of course, the prince did not know that she was a princess, and he put her to work in the kitchen among the pots and pans.

Some time later the prince decided to give a series of three balls. He invited all the princesses from nearby kingdoms. From among them he planned to choose a bride. Briar Rose was so curious about the ball that she opened the golden nutshell (for she had remembered to take it with her) and drew out the gown made of the sun's rays. When she appeared in the ballroom, the prince was fascinated by her. But she only stayed a short while and then fled back to the kitchen.

One day while she was bringing some soup to the prince, she dropped in a golden ring. That night the prince gave a second ball, and Briar Rose went, dressed in her gown of moonlight. The prince was even more enchanted with her this time, but again she slipped away before he could find out who she was. The next day, while preparing the prince's wine, she dropped in a golden locket. That night the last ball was held, and the princess appeared in her gown of velvet night and stars, and this time the prince fell madly in love with her. Again she escaped before he could find her out.

By this time the prince was beginning to wonder who had been preparing his meals. He questioned the cook, and putting two and two together, came to the conclusion that the kitchen maid must be the beautiful girl at the ball. They were soon married, and of course they lived happily ever after.

In the 19th century Jacob and Wilhelm Grimm adapted fairy tales from German folklore.

HANSEL AND GRETEL

Once upon a time there was a very poor woodcutter who had two children, a boy named Hansel and a girl named Gretel. Their mother had died and the father had married again. Their new mother was a harsh woman, and since times were bad and food scarce, she considered the two children a burden.

Things went from bad to worse, and one day the poor woodcutter found there were only two loaves of bread left in the house. Sadly, he agreed with the stepmother that the two children would have to be taken out into the woods and left to fend for themselves, so that there would be only half as many mouths to feed. But Hansel overheard this, and when all were asleep, he slipped out of the house and filled up his pocket with bright pebbles. The next day as they traveled through the woods, the clever Hansel left a trail of pebbles. And when their parents had left them, the children followed the trail home.

The stepmother pretended to be glad to see them and scolded them for getting lost. The father was truly glad. Things went well for a while, but soon times grew worse than ever, and the woodcutter was told by his wife that now there was only one loaf of bread in the house, and the children would have to be left in the woods again. Hansel heard this, and that night he tried to slip out to gather

45

more pebbles. But the door was locked this time. When their father gave them a crust of bread for their noon meal in the woods, Hansel broke it up and left a trail of breadcrumbs instead.

This time, however, things did not work out so well, for birds ate the trail of breadcrumbs, and the children were really lost. They wandered for days, until at last they found themselves before a wonderful house made of gingerbread, chocolate, and cake. Hungrily they began to nibble at the house, when the door opened

and an ugly witch appeared. "Come inside," she said, "and I'll give you all you want to eat."

The children obeyed, and quick as a wink the old witch grabbed Hansel and threw him into a cage. "There you'll stay, you greedy boy, until you're nice and plump, and then I'll roast you for my dinner." But the old hag could not see very well, and each day when she reached in to see if Hansel was plump enough, he would hand her a thin stick to feel. The witch kept wondering why all her food

47

meal of Hansel's breadcrumb trail, and they were all twittering and pointing to the roof of the witch's house. There Hansel found a treasure of gems—diamonds, pearls, rubies, and emeralds. He scooped them up, and followed the birds, who, feeling a bit guilty about having eaten the bread crumbs, guided the children home.

Their father embraced them happily. The stepmother, however, only looked sourly at the children, for she had thought she was rid of them. Even the jewels did not help, and she soon packed her bags and left. But the others lived happily ever after.

didn't seem to fatten Hansel at all. Finally, the witch grew tired of all this and decided to cook Hansel, fat or thin. She thought she might just as well eat Gretel, too, and have a two-course dinner. She planned to trick the girl into lighting the fire, and then push her into it.

But Gretel was no fool and saw through the witch's trick. Playing stupid, she said: "Well, I really don't know how to light a fire. Would you show me please?" The witch furiously pushed her aside and bent over to light the fire herself. At that point Gretel neatly pushed the witch into the oven, slammed the door, and lit the fire. And the witch howled and kicked as she was roasted to a turn.

Gretel quickly freed Hansel, who praised her quick thinking. They kissed each other and danced and laughed, for they had never thought to get away alive. Suddenly, there was a noise outside, and the children saw a flock of birds. It was the same birds who had made a

THE SEVEN RAVENS

In a faraway land there was a good king who had seven strapping sons. But one thing saddened the king and queen: they wished for a little girl. The king's wizard predicted that girl would be born when seven ravens cried.

Some time passed and there was great rejoicing, for a princess had been born. The king sent his seven sons to get some water from a magic brook. A few drops of this water would make the princess—who was named Elizabeth—grow into a beautiful maiden. The seven brothers flew as fast as the wind. But they stopped to chat with some elves, and wasted so much time that the king became furious.

"May those lazy sons of mine be turned into ravens!" he cried. As soon as the words were spoken, the king saw flying overhead seven croaking ravens with tiny gold crowns on their heads. Thus the prophecy had come true.

Elizabeth grew up into a beautiful maiden, even without the magic water. One day, when she had scolded a careless servant, the servant told her spitefully that it was her fault that her brothers had been turned into ravens. Grief-stricken, Elizabeth set out to find her brothers. She searched far and wide, but it was hopeless. Then one day a star, the brightest in the sky, took pity on her. The star offered her a gold key. "Take this, Elizabeth. It is a magic key. Go to the crystal mountain, where you will find a

tiny door. Open it and you will see a dwarf. And then you will find your brothers."

The young princess did as she was told. But, alas! When she got to the tiny door, she dropped the key and lost it. Without hesitating, she cut off her small finger and used it as a key to open the door.

When the door opened, Elizabeth found herself face to face with a dwarf, who was very busy setting seven plates with breadcrumbs and seven glasses with water. Elizabeth, who was very hungry, ate all the breadcrumbs and drank all the water. But into the last glass she dropped a golden ring that her mother had given her to keep her safe. Then she hid herself, for she heard someone coming.

In a moment seven large black ravens flew in, and great was their surprise and their fury when they found the platters clean and the glasses empty.

"Who has eaten from my plate?" asked one of the ravens angrily.

"Who has drunk from my glass?" asked another of the ravens suspiciously.

"And who has dropped our mother's golden ring into my glass?" asked a third raven with wonder in his voice.

"It was I! It was I, your little sister!" exclaimed Elizabeth as she jumped out of her hiding place and ran to embrace the brothers whom she had never seen.

As she embraced them she wept sad tears at the thought that her handsome brothers must live as ravens. And then a strange thing happened. As Eliabeth's tears fell on the seven ravens' feathers, they gradually changed, and soon the seven birds were once again the seven strapping brothers. For her tears had broken the magic spell.

RAPUNZEL

Once upon a time there lived a man and his wife who, after many years, were finally expecting a child. One day the wife saw some delicious vegetables in the next-door garden, which belonged to a witch. The wife developed a great desire for them, and refused to eat anything else. Her husband, fearing that she would die, sneaked next door to gather some of the vegetables. But he was caught by the witch. In exchange for the vegetables, she made him promise to give her his child as soon as it should be born.

51

When the child was born, it turned out to be a beautiful girl. The witch took her away and later put her in a high tower with no stairs and no door. There was only one way to reach the top. When the witch wished to enter, she would call: "Rapunzel, Rapunzel! Let down your golden hair!" And Rapunzel would then undo her long hair, and the old witch would climb up it.

One day a handsome prince was passing and, hearing the lonely Rapunzel

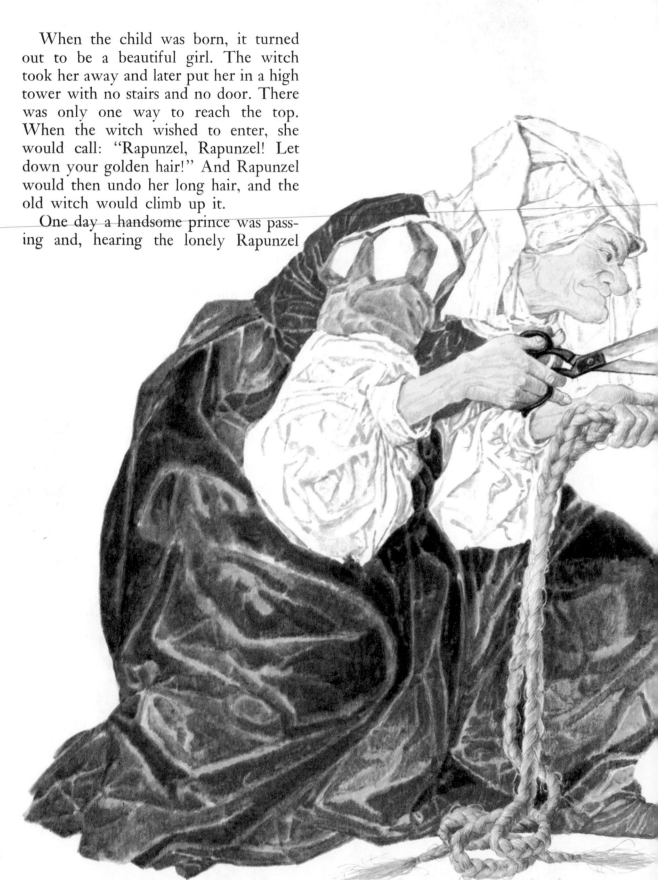

singing to herself, he fell in love with the owner of the beautiful voice. Longing to see her, he waited by the tower and soon saw how the witch climbed up. When she had left, he called out the magic words and did the same. The two soon fell in love. The prince left a silken ladder for Rapunzel's escape from the tower, but it was discovered by the enraged witch. She cut off Rapunzel's hair and sent her away to a desert island. When the prince arrived, the witch let down the cut braids. When he climbed to the top, she pushed him off, and he fell in some thorns that pierced his eyes.

The blind prince roamed the world until, one day, he heard Rapunzel singing. The beautiful sound guided him to the desert island. The sweethearts embraced, but when Rapunzel saw what had happened to the prince, she wept. Two glistening tears fell onto the prince's blind eyes, and he was able to see again. Then he took Rapunzel to his own kingdom where they married and lived happily ever after.

THE MAGIC TABLE

Once upon a time—and, of course, most good stories must begin with "once upon a time"—there was a poor tailor who had three sons. When they grew to manhood, the tailor was greatly perplexed as to how they were to earn their living. So he decided to send them out into the world, each to learn a different trade.

The oldest son he apprenticed to a carpenter. An apprentice usually works for little or no money while he learns his trade. Well, the oldest son learned his trade well, and the carpenter became so fond of him that after he had finished his apprenticeship, he gave him a wooden table as a gift.

The table was nothing much to look at, and the oldest son was somewhat disappointed. "It seems like a very ordinary table," he said, "and not especially well made, either."

The carpenter smiled. "I agree that it doesn't look like much," he said. "But it is really a very special table. All you have

54

to do is say 'Table Set!' and the table will suddenly be loaded with a complete feast.'' The young apprentice thought: "That means I'll have enough to eat for the rest of my life, and I'll never have to pay for a meal." And off he went with his table.

One day he decided to return home to pay his father a visit. On the way he stopped at a tavern. It was crowded and there was no food left in the kitchen. So the young man said "Table Set!" and the table set up a special feast. The innkeep-

er, a dishonest fellow, so envied the young man his table that during the night he stole it and replaced it with one that looked the same.

Not realizing what had happened, the young carpenter set off next day with the substitute table. When he reached home, he told his father of his marvelous possession. "Invite all our friends and our relatives," said the carpenter, "and we'll order a special banquet for them."

The tailor did so. But when the time came for the meal and the young man

55

ordered the table to set, it remained empty, to the embarrassment of the guests and the shame of the young man.

Meanwhile, the second son had learned the miller's trade. When his apprenticeship was over, his employer gave him a donkey as a gift. "Just put the donkey on a cloth and say "Bricklebrit" and this good animal will spout gold coins from its mouth." Rich and happy, the young miller set out to see the world, until he too began to miss his father. On the way home he stopped at the same tavern where his older brother's table had been stolen. But since he had no way of knowing this, when it came time to pay his supper bill, he merely said the magic word to the magic donkey. Needless to say, during the night the innkeeper replaced the priceless beast with an ordinary donkey.

When the young man arrived home, he gave the animal to his father, saying: "Invite all our relatives and friends. There's gold enough for all!"

But it was the same story again—disappointment and shame.

The third brother had been apprenticed to a potter. His apprenticeship took a little longer, and he only learned of his brothers' misfortunes by letter. When the time came for him to leave, he was given a stick. "It is a magic stick," explained the potter. "All you have to do is say 'Stick Beat!' and the stick will strike away as hard as you please, and it won't stop until you order it to do so."

The potter decided to use his gift to avenge his brothers. Arriving at the same tavern, he told the dishonest owner about his magic stick, and then lay down and pretended to sleep, keeping one eye open. Spotting the innkeeper stealing the stick, he yelled: "Stick Beat!" and he didn't order it to stop until the innkeeper had returned the table and the donkey.

The third son returned home with all three gifts, and, like his brothers before, invited all their friends and relatives. This time there was food, drink, and gold for all. And they lived happily ever after, fed by the table, enriched by the donkey, and protected by the stick.

THE BREMEN TOWN MUSICIANS

Once there was an old donkey whose master had decided to do away with him. But the donkey ran away when he learned of the scheme. He set out for Bremen in the hope of finding work with the town band. Along the way, he met a dog that was too old to hunt, and a cat too old to catch mice. They, too, had masters who wanted to get rid of them, and so they had run off.

"Come with me to Bremen and we'll join the musicians," said the donkey. The cat and dog were happy to join the donkey, and the three friends continued along the road. Soon they came across a rooster who was squawking because his mistress was planning to cook him in the morning as part of a holiday celebration. "Instead of squawking, why not come with us to Bremen," suggested the three friends. The rooster gladly accepted their offer.

The road to Bremen was a long one, and they decided to spend the night in the forest. The rooster climbed into a tree and from his perch spotted a light in a nearby house. He told his friends about it, and they decided to go there to look for a place to sleep and something to eat.

But when they got to the house and looked in the window, they found it was a thieves' hideout. As the robbers were just sitting down to dinner, the animals

57

hatched a plan. The dog jumped onto the donkey's back, the cat climbed on top of the dog, and the rooster perched on the cat's head. At a signal, they began to bray, bark, meeow, and crow. The noise frightened the robbers, who ran out the door. Laughing heartily, the four friends sat down at the table and ate the food.

When they finished eating, they all found places to stretch out and sleep. Meanwhile, the leader of the robber band saw that the house was dark again and sent one of his men to investigate. The robbers' scout crept into the house, but it was too dark to see anything. He mistook the cat's shiny eyes for glowing coals and tried to use them to light a match.

This enraged the cat, who jumped at him and scratched his face. The robber let out a yell and tried to run. But he tripped over the dog, who bit him on the leg. As he hobbled by the haystack where the donkey was sleeping, he got a swift kick from that animal's hind legs. At this point, the rooster let out a loud, piercing squawk.

The frightened and bruised robber ran like the wind back to his friends. In a trembling voice, he told the leader, "There's a witch in the house who jumped on me and scratched my face. When I tried to get away, a man stabbed me in the leg with his knife. The next thing I know some big monster with long ears smacked me with a club. Then someone shouted 'Get that bandit,' so I ran back here as fast as my feet could carry me."

From that day on, the robbers never again came near the house. As for the animals, they were so happy there that they never did get to Bremen.

THE KING OF THE GOLDEN MOUNTAIN

There was once a rich merchant who lost all of his goods in a shipwreck. Later, as he sadly traveled home, he met a little man who told him: "I promise you more riches than you ever had before. However, you must agree that 12 years from now you will bring me the first thing you meet when you reach your home."

Since the merchant thought his dog would be first to greet him, he agreed. But when he got home, it was his infant son, who had just learned to walk, who ran out to meet him. The merchant remembered his promise and became frightened—especially when he found a bundle of money waiting for him in the house.

As time passed, the merchant worried even more. When his son asked him what was wrong, he told him the story. "Don't worry, Father," the boy said. "Everything will be all right." Then the boy went to church to ask for a special blessing.

When it came time to keep the bargain, father and son went to meet the little man. But the little man didn't want the boy, because of the blessing. Instead, he cast him adrift on a river in a small boat. The boat capsized, and it appeared that the boy had drowned.

However, the young man had held onto the underside of the boat and was carried safely to shore. He landed near an enchanted castle, where he met a snake

60

that was really a young girl under an evil spell. She told the boy he could free her if he withstood three days of torture by the little man without crying out in pain.

The boy agreed and for three days he took the punishment without making a sound. Afterward, the snake turned into a beautiful princess and married the boy. And that's how the young man became the King of the Golden Mountain.

THE SHOEMAKER AND THE ELVES

This is the story of a poor shoemaker and his wife. Business had been very bad for the shoemaker until finally he had nothing left except one last piece of leather. It was just enough to make a single pair of shoes.

Before going to bed one evening, the shoemaker cut the pieces of leather and left them on his workbench. He planned to finish the shoes in the morning. Then he said his prayers, put his future in God's hands, and went to sleep.

In the morning, when he went to his workbench, his eyes widened in surprise. There before him was a beautiful pair of finished shoes. Every stich was just right, and the shoes were perfect in every way. As the shoemaker looked at them in disbelief, a rich merchant came into the shop. He saw the shoes and immediately bought them for a handsome price.

Still overwhelmed by his good fortune, the shoemaker took the money and bought enough leather to make two pairs of shoes. He cut the leather into pieces and left them on the workbench as he had the night before. In the morning, when he went to his bench to finish the shoes, he found that the same thing had happened. Two pairs of perfect shoes were waiting for him. Once again he sold the shoes and bought more leather. And again he found the shoes were finished when he woke up the next morning.

The same miracle happened over and over again. Soon the shoemaker was once more earning a good living. One evening shortly before Christmas, the shoemaker again laid out the leather pieces on his work bench. But this time his wife suggested that they stay awake to find out who was making the beautiful shoes. So the two of them hid behind a curtain and waited patiently.

As the clock struck midnight, two little elves—naked as jaybirds—entered the room. They sat down at the workbench and began to sew the pieces of leather quickly and skillfully. They worked without letup until the shoes were finished. Then they put them on the table and left as quietly as they had come.

When they were gone, the wife said to the shoemaker: "We should do something to reward those wonderful little elves. After all, they saved us from the poorhouse. Since they don't seem to have any clothes, I'm going to make them some as a Christmas gift."

"That's a good idea," agreed the shoemaker. "And I will make a pair of fine shoes for each of them."

By Christmas Eve everything was ready. That night the shoemaker and his wife left the little clothes and shoes on the workbench instead of the usual pieces of leather. Then they took their places behind the curtain and waited for the elves. At exactly midnight, the elves arrived and playfully somersaulted onto the bench.

To their surprise and delight, they found the clothes waiting for them. The elves got dressed and began to sing and dance. In fact, they danced all around— on the floor, over the workbench, even up into the loft. Finally, they danced right out of the shop, and were never seen again after that day. But the shoemaker and his wife lived happily ever after.

Hans Christian Andersen (1805–1875), the famous Danish author of many lovely stories and fairy tales.

THE LITTLE MERMAID

Once upon a time there was a castle located far away in the deepest and bluest part of the ocean. Inside the coral walls of this castle lived the King of the Sea. The king had six mermaid daughters, with long fish tails, and they lived in the castle with their grandmother and the king. All of the daughters were pretty, but the youngest was the most beautiful of all.

They all lived happily together on the floor of the ocean. Sometimes their grandmother, a dear old mermaid, told them stories about life in the ocean and on land. The youngest mermaid was especially interested in these stories. She dreamed of seeing these places herself. Grandmother promised that when each of them reached her fifteenth birthday she could visit the land and see the world of men.

And that's just what happened. One by one the mermaids went to visit the world on land. Eventually they returned to their ocean kingdom. All but one decided that they preferred their world to man's. The one exception was the youngest and prettiest of them all. For she had fallen in love with a handsome young prince.

She told her grandmother what had happened and the wise old mermaid replied, "Poor dear, you can't marry him, because you are a mermaid and he is a man. You are a creature of the sea and he is a creature of the land."

But the little mermaid was too much in love to heed these words. Her heart was broken and she began to hate herself because she was a mermaid. All day and night she wept for her prince. Finally, her grandmother allowed her to go to the Witch of the Sea to ask for help.

The witch was sympathetic. "I shall give you human form and a pair of legs," said the witch. "But if you don't marry your prince, you will die and become foam on the waves. In return for my favor, I want your voice."

The little mermaid protested. "But if you take my voice, how will I talk to the prince?"

"Your graceful ways will be words enough to win the prince's heart," answered the witch.

The little mermaid soon found herself on land with human form but no voice. She went straight to the prince, who was taken by her beauty. But when he found out that she was mute, he took pity on her and treated her like a sister. The poor little mermaid could not tell him that what she wanted most of all was to be his bride. Still, she was happy enough just to be near her beloved prince. For a while, everything went well.

Then, one day, the prince decided to marry a princess from a neighboring

kingdom. The little mermaid was grief-stricken. When her sisters and grandmother learned of her misfortune, they wanted to do something. With the help of the Witch of the Sea, they came up with a plan. The little mermaid was given a special knife sent by the Witch of the Sea. She was told to plunge the knife into the prince's heart while he slept. If she did that, her life would be spared and she would become a mermaid once more.

On the appointed day the little mermaid crept into the prince's room and raised the dagger over his heart. But just as she was about to strike, the prince opened his eyes and smiled at her. "What is it my little sister?" he asked sweetly. "Are you trying to tell me that some danger threatens me? Have no fear, I can defend us both if necessary. . . ."

The little mermaid could not bear to hear any more. Her heart melted. She fled from the room, knowing that she must soon die. By dawn, she felt the change coming on. Just as the witch had threatened, she was turning into foam—the beautiful white foam that caps the waves as they roll over the endless blue sea.

THE RED SHOES

Karen was a little orphan girl who was so poor she went barefoot all year round. One day a kind lady adopted her and raised her as her daughter. Over the years Karen grew into a beautiful girl. Finally the time came for her Holy Communion and her foster mother took Karen out to buy a pair of new shoes.

Now Karen was very self-centered. She wanted a pair of red shoes like those worn by the queen's daughter. When she saw a pair in the shoemaker's window,

she begged her foster mother to buy them for her. The lady's eyesight was poor, so she bought the shoes not realizing that they were red dancing shoes.

During the Holy Communion ceremony, Karen admired her beautiful red shoes instead of paying attention to the service. The shocked churchgoers told her mother that the shoes were dancing shoes and Karen was forbidden to wear them to church again. But the following Sunday, her confirmation day, Karen disobeyed her mother. Once again she put on her red dancing shoes. Karen was stopped at the church gate by an evil-looking man leaning on a crutch. "What lovely dancing shoes you have on," he said with a devilish laugh. "Let me shine them for you." As he shined them, the strange man tapped the soles and said "Stay on her feet, little shoes, and make her dance." And then he disappeared.

Karen spent most of the time in church admiring her shoes, just as she had done the previous week. When she left the church, she again saw the man. "Dance, shoes, dance!" he ordered, and suddenly Karen began to dance. She danced so fast and wildly she couldn't stop. Fortunately her mother's coachman grabbed her and pulled off the shoes. Her mother warned her never to wear them again.

Time went by and Karen's mother became old and fell ill. But instead of caring for her mother, who lay on her deathbed, Karen decided to go to a party. And even though she knew it was wrong, she put on her red dancing shoes. No sooner were they on her feet than she was forced to dance. The shoes made her dance every which way but never the way she wanted to go. Karen tried to pull them off, but they seemed to be glued to her feet.

Poor Karen danced for days and days. Finally she danced past the little church where she had been confirmed. She wanted to go inside and ask forgiveness for being so selfish, but an angel with a flaming sword blocked her way. "Go back," said the angel. "In your silly pride you allowed your mother to die alone. Your punishment shall be to dance until you are old and withered."

"Have mercy!" Karen pleaded, but her shoes were already carrying her away. Later, as she danced by a neighbor's house, she called out to him, "Please pull off my shoes, I beg you, so that I can stop dancing." The neighbor carried out her request. He grabbed her and pulled off her little red dancing shoes and they danced away into the woods. Poor Karen's feet were tired and sore from all the dancing. But the kindly neighbor took her into his house and bathed and bandaged her feet.

Afterward Karen went to church and prayed to be forgiven. From then on she stopped being selfish and performed many kind deeds for other people. But every now and then she would think of her red dancing shoes. Years later, when she was a very old lady, the angel of the Lord appeared again. He told her that because she had led such a good life she was forgiven. At last she was at peace.

THE EMPEROR'S NEW CLOTHES

One day two weavers were brought before the emperor of a great land. This emperor was very fond of beautiful clothes. In fact he spent so much money on clothes that he hardly had anything left for his kingdom. Now the emperor had heard that these two weavers could makes clothes having special qualities.

"I have been told that you weave a beautiful fabric," the king said to the weavers after they had bowed to him.

"It is true your majesty," said the first weaver. "But that isn't the only reason why it is special."

"What other reason can there be?" demanded the emperor.

"You see, your majesty," the second weaver explained. "Clothes made of our fabric are invisible to people who are fools or liars."

"That is truly amazing," remarked the king. "With such clothes, I will be able to find out who are the fools and who are the wise men in my kingdom. I command you to make me a full suit of clothes."

70

So the weavers immediately went to work. They were given gold thread, looms, and a room to work in. All of the king's ministers and servants were put at their disposal. The weavers were told to make the clothes in time for a great procession that was to take place in a few days.

As you may have guessed, the weavers were a couple of swindlers looking for an easy way to make money. All day they sat at their looms pretending to make the king's suit. Only, of course, the looms were empty. After a few days, the king sent one of his ministers to see how the work was going.

"Isn't it beautiful?" one of the weavers asked the minister, pointing to the empty loom. The minister couldn't see a thing, but he thought quickly to himself, "If I can't see it I must be a fool, and if the emperor finds out, he'll fire me." So instead he told them, "It is truly the most splendid fabric I have ever seen. The patterns and colors are breathtaking." And he went back and told the king the same thing.

Day after day the weavers worked. They ordered more gold thread and materials, which they put in their bags, and they received more money from the emperor as well. By this time the emperor couldn't resist going to see the fabric himself. Naturally he saw nothing when he looked at the looms. But like his minister, he thought "My goodness! I don't see anything but empty space. But I mustn't let on or the word will spread that the emperor is a fool." So he too lied. "Weavers," he said, "you have outdone yourselves. Your fabric is beyond my wildest dreams."

A short time later the weavers declared that they were finished. They pretended to fit the imaginary coat, pants, and cape to the emperor and then announced, "Your majesty is the best-dressed emperor in all the world." After receiving their last payment, they quickly disappeared.

That very day the emperor led the great procession through the streets of the city. The emperor thought he was dressed in beautiful clothes. But in fact he had on nothing more than his underwear. As he walked through the streets, the people gasped. Everyone could see that the emperor had no clothes. But no one would say anything for fear of being called a fool. So they all expressed admiration for the emperor's new clothes. "What beautiful clothes the emperor has on," one would say, and others would shake their heads in agreement.

All except one little child, who suddenly cried out, "But he hasn't got any clothes on!" And the people realized it was true, and soon they were all laughing and shouting, "He has nothing on! The emperor has no clothes!" The emperor, who had been feeling a bit chilly, knew then that he had been tricked. But he would not admit it before his subjects. He pretended not to hear them. Instead he walked on, more proudly than before, as if dressed in his finest robes.

THE LITTLE MATCH GIRL

It was Christmas Eve and very, very cold. The streets of the city were covered with a soft, thick blanket of snow, so soft and thick that the passers-by sank in deeply with each step. The dogs, frolicking in it, sank in with all four paws till the snow reached their throats. But, as dogs will, they jumped right out again . . . and fell right in again. They made a funny sight, those dogs, and the little girl amused herself watching them.

The little girl was a match girl, a seller of boxes of matches. Her father, a very poor man, had sent her out into the street to try to earn a few pennies, for they had so little food that even those pennies would be welcome.

But this evening, so busy and jolly for most people, was not a happy one for the little girl. For although she had been

standing in the cold snow for hours, she had not yet sold a single box of matches. As she gazed into the brightly-lit store windows, filled with so many good things, she tried to forget the hunger pains in her stomach and the cold that gripped her bare feet.

The little girl felt terribly tired and cold, and she huddled down between two houses to try to get warm. She let her thoughts roam and day-dreamed of a house with a warm, roaring fire in the fireplace. Then she thought, "Why not light just one match to warm myself? My father won't begrudge me one match, and perhaps my stepmother won't notice." She lit the match. It lasted only a

second but it made a comforting glow and gave a little warmth. She lit another, and another. Then as if in a dream, an enormous table appeared before her, loaded with good things to eat, sweet-smelling and delicious. And the table seemed so close that the little match girl felt as if she could reach out her hand and take a chicken leg. How she loved chicken. . . .

"Grandma, Oh, Grandma!" exclaimed the girl suddenly in a high voice. "Why did you go away without me? Why did

you leave me here all alone? If only you knew how cold it is . . . and how my stepmother beats me now that you're gone. Grandma, is it really true that you are in Paradise?"

By now the little match girl had used up all her matches, the matches that she had hoped to sell, but that no one wanted to buy.

"You know, Grandma," the little girl went on, her voice even higher, for now she was delirious with fever, "I have an idea. Why don't you take me with you? Please take me with you! Give me your hand and let me come along with you. I know there will be food to eat there and a place to warm myself. Yes? Did you say yes?"

As the snow continued to fall it covered the body of the little match girl with soft, white flakes. The little girl lay there stiff and cold, as if asleep. But she had a smile on her pale lips, for she had seen her grandmother reaching out her hand to her, ready to take the little girl with her.

THE ELEVEN
WILD SWANS

In a beautiful castle in a faraway land there once lived a king and queen with their eleven sons and one lovely daughter. Fortune smiled on the royal family. Nothing seemed to mar their happiness until one sad day the queen took ill and died. The king, not wishing his children to grow up without a mother, soon took a new wife. From that day on misfortune settled upon the once happy family. First the eleven handsome princes disappeared mysteriously, and soon afterwards the cruel stepmother, jealous of the king's love for his daughter, forced him to send the beautiful princess away from the court.

One evening while the banished princess was wandering about sadly wondering what would become of her, a strange whirring sound caught her attention. She looked up, and there in the sky she saw eleven beautiful swans each wearing a small golden crown. Her curiosity was aroused by the lovely creatures, so she followed them to a nearby brook. There, to her great amazement, she saw them change before her eyes into her eleven missing brothers.

The princes were delighted to find their sister safe and sound, and at once began to explain their fate.

"When the sun shines in the sky," they said, "we fly as swans. When evening falls we become men again. That is why we must be careful never to be in flight after the sun sets, otherwise we would surely fall to the ground and be killed. We live on a distant island, and the journey to reach it is long. We must rest our wings often on our way, and that is why we have stopped at this brook."

When the princess heard their story,

she begged them to take her with them to their secret island. So the next morning the swans placed their widespread wings close together and carried the princess, safe as though she were in a cradle, high into the sky. And just as the sun sank below the horizon and night began to fall, they reached their island home.

The princess was desperate to find a way to release her brothers from the spell they were under. She thought and thought but she could find no solution.

One day the Good Fairy appeared before her. "I will tell you," said the fairy, "how you can save your brothers. But you must listen carefully and follow my instructions exactly, otherwise the young princes will be doomed to death. In a grotto close to the garden there is a bed of sharp nettles. You must gather the nettles with your own hands and stamp them with your own feet. From the thread you must spin eleven cloaks and throw them over your brothers' shoulders. Only then

will they be saved. But you must be careful not to utter one single word while you perform this difficult task. If you break your silence, your brothers will surely die."

Then the Good Fairy disappeared, and immediately the princess began to pluck the nettles she would need for the eleven cloaks. Many days and many nights she labored, until her hands and feet were sore and bleeding. But when her brothers pitied her and asked why she was toiling at her task, she remembered the warning of the Good Fairy and never once did she speak.

One day as the brothers were flying through the sky, a handsome young prince passed by the grotto. As soon as he saw the beautiful princess he fell in love with her. And though she became his bride, she continued to gather her nettles and never spoke a single word.

At first the prince overlooked his wife's strange habits. But evil gossipers started to whisper that the princess was a witch, and before long the prince began to believe them. The bridegroom finally decided that his wife must be put to death. He listened to the advice of his counselors and began to make the arrangements. Just as she was completing the last sleeve of the eleventh cloak, the princess, still sad and silent, was led from the palace.

But as she was about to die, eleven beautiful swans flew down from the sky to rescue her. She had just time enough to finish the final sleeve and throw the cloaks over her brothers' shoulders. As soon as she had done so, the eleven swans turned into handsome young princes, just as the Good Fairy had promised.

Such rejoicing throughout the land! The happy prince returned to his castle with the princess and her brothers, and all of them lived there blissfully for the rest of their lives.

THE PRINCESS AND THE PEA

What a downpour! There hadn't been a storm like this for years and years—for hundreds of years—to be exact. All the animals in the forest ran as fast as they could to seek shelter. The rain poured from the heavens. Bolts of lightning lit the warm summer sky. The crackling of the thunder shook the entire valley.

In the great castle high on the hill lived a king, a queen, and their son, a handsome young prince. The prince's parents had long ago decided that their son should marry a princess. Not just any princess, mind you, but a real honest-to-goodness princess. The young prince had searched all over the world for just such a girl. But he was unable to find one. He returned to the castle in the midst of the storm to tell his parents the sad news. As he told the king and queen of his unsuccessful travels, a crack of lightning streaked through the dark sky. Just then, a knock, knock, knock sounded on the castle door. The old king took leave of his wife and son, picked up a large lantern and went to see who would be knocking on his door in such a terrible storm.

Imagine his surprise when he opened the door and saw a young girl standing before him. What a sight she was! Water was streaming down her face, and her poor clothes were soaked and torn. But what was even more surprising was that she told the old king that she was a princess! The king, upon hearing such news, hurried the young girl into the

79

warmth of the castle.

When the king introduced the princess to his wife, the old queen exclaimed, "A princess? This . . . this . . . ragamuffin? Nonsense!"

"Your majesty," said the young girl, "I am a princess—a real princess. And after a good night's rest, I'll explain to you why I am not dressed in my royal robes."

All the while the handsome prince stood aside and gazed lovingly at the young girl. He drew his mother aside and whispered, "I don't care whether she is a real princess or not—I'm going to marry her!"

"Quiet," said his mother. "You may marry only a true princess. And we'll soon find out if this girl is indeed of royal birth. Just leave things to me."

The old queen sent for the cook and told her to bring some hot broth for their unexpected guest. The girl ate the soup and then asked if a room might be prepared so that she could rest for the night. The old queen said that she personally would see to it that a room was made ready . . . a room fit for a princess!

"I beg you, your majesty, please give me a very soft mattress," said the young girl. "Otherwise I will be unable to sleep." The queen hurried to the royal bedchamber. She took off all of the bed clothes and placed one tiny pea on the bottom boards of the bed. Then she took 20 mattresses and put them on top of the pea. The queen sent for the girl. "Goodnight, princess! Pleasant dreams!" she said as the exhausted girl, with great effort, threw herself on the huge bed.

The next morning the king, queen, and prince waited at the breakfast table for the girl to appear. They waited nearly an hour. At last the poor girl walked sleepily into the room. "Good morning," said the queen. "Did you sleep well?"

"Did I sleep well?" the girl replied. "Why I didn't sleep a wink all night. I tossed and turned for hours."

"Whatever was the matter?" asked the queen.

"The bed . . . something was wrong with the bed," answered the girl. "I was lying on something so hard that I'm black and blue from the tip of my toes to the top of my head. Just look at me. Why, I've never been so uncomfortable."

"My dear child," exclaimed the queen, "now I can see that you are a real princess. Only a true princess with tender, delicate skin could have felt a pea hidden under 20 mattresses."

So the prince took the young girl for his wife. They lived happily ever after with the old king and queen in the castle overlooking the village. The townspeople

were thrilled with their new princess, and she with them.

The pea—the famous green pea—became part of the royal treasury. Many people thought that it was even more precious than the crown jewels because it had the power to bring about such happiness.

And today—yes, even today—that very same pea is still on display in the royal museum. That is, if no one has taken it!

THE LITTLE TIN SOLDIER

Once upon a time there were 25 little tin soldiers. They all looked exactly alike because they had been made from the same batch of tin. The soldiers all carried rifles on their shoulders, and they stood tall and proud. But one soldier was different from all the others. He was the last soldier to be molded from the batch of tin. And since there was barely enough tin left, this little soldier was given only one leg. But he stood as straight and tall on his one leg as the others did on both legs.

All of these toy soldiers belonged to a little boy. He kept them on a shelf along with his other playthings. One of the most unusual toys was a cardboard castle. A paper doll, dressed in a beautiful white tutu, with a golden star pinned in her hair, lived in the castle. The little doll was a ballerina. Her arms were held gracefully over her head, and one of her legs was pointed high in the air. In fact, the leg was raised so high that the little tin soldier was unable to see it. He thought that the ballerina, like himself, had only one leg. In a very short time, the soldier fell in love with the paper doll.

But alas, it was not a long romance. Living on the same shelf as the soldier and the ballerina, was the jack-in-the-box. He too was in love with the paper doll. One day, the jack-in-the-box became very angry. He jumped out of his box with a start, knocking the little tin soldier out of the window. The poor soldier went flying through the air and landed with a crash on the sidewalk.

He was found by two young boys. Thinking that the toy soldier was broken, the boys put him in a paper boat and set it sailing down a nearby brook. The water became very rough, and in no time at all the poor soldier felt his boat sinking. He thought of the beautiful paper ballerina and that he would never see her again. All of a sudden the soldier was swallowed by a giant fish. How dark it was! But the soldier was brave. Shortly the fish began to flop about. Then it lay very still.

Time passed slowly for the tin soldier. Then one day he saw a knife blade cutting into the belly of the fish. He heard someone exclaim "Look! Here's the tin soldier!" What a surprise! The fish had been caught and sold to the cook in the very same house where the little soldier's adventures began.

And the best part of all was that he was put back on the shelf beside his beloved ballerina. But again his happiness was not to last. One day, for no reason

at all, the little boy who owned the toys threw the tin soldier into the stove. Through the flames the soldier saw the ballerina weeping. Just then a strong breeze came through the window, blowing the paper ballerina into the stove. She disappeared in the flames in no time while the little tin soldier slowly melted away.

The next morning the maid came to clean the ashes out of the stove. All that she found was a little tin heart and the scorched star of the ballerina, black as a piece of coal.

THE TINDER BOX

One day a soldier returning from war met an old witch near a hollow tree trunk. "I shall make you rich," said the witch. "If you'll go down into the tree trunk, you'll find three large dogs at the bottom, each one guarding a chest filled with money. Take all the coins you want, but bring me an old tinder box you will find down there."

The soldier agreed. The witch tied a long cord around his waist and lowered him down the tree trunk. Sure enough, it was just as the witch said it would be. The soldier filled his pockets and boots with coins, and, with the tinder box in hand, yelled to the witch to pull him up.

But once he was above ground, he refused to give the tinder box to the witch. The soldier left her angry and grumbling.

Since he was so rich, the soldier lived like a king. But he spent his money so quickly that soon it was all gone. He didn't even have enough left to buy a candle. Then the soldier remembered that the tinder box had a small candle taper attached to it. He rubbed the box to light the taper, and, as if by magic, the three dogs appeared. "How may we help you, my lord?" asked the animals. Astonished, the soldier ordered the dogs to make him rich. The animals disappeared, but in an instant they returned with bags full of coins.

Now it happened that in the same city there lived a king with a very beautiful

daughter. The princess, however, was held prisoner by her father in the castle. Long before, a wizard told the king that his daughter would one day marry a common soldier. To prevent her from doing this, the king kept his daughter under lock and key.

The soldier heard about the princess and one night sent one of his dogs to fetch her. The trusty animal returned with the sleeping princess. The soldier, seeing how beautiful the princess was, fell in love with her immediately. He kissed her gently so as not to awaken her and then ordered the dog to return her to the castle.

The next morning the princess told her parents that in her dreams she had been carried off by a dog and kissed by a soldier. The queen was furious. That night she tied a sack of grain to her daughter's waist and cut a hole in the sack. If indeed the dream turned out to be a true story, the king could follow the trail left by the falling grain.

And that's exactly what happened! That night the princess was again carried off by the dog. The next morning the king and his guards followed the trail of grain and captured the soldier. As he was being led to prison, the soldier asked if he might carry his tinder box. As soon as the guards gave it to him, the soldier rubbed the box. The three dogs appeared, causing wonder and panic among the crowd and the court. The king was so astounded that he ordered the soldier freed and gave him his daughter's hand in marriage.

THE SONG OF HIAWATHA

There is an old Indian legend that tells of a great hero who appeared among the many North American Indian tribes. He wanted to help his fellow tribesmen and teach them the arts of peace and good fellowship. The Indian hero was called Hiawatha.

Shortly after Hiawatha was born, his mother died. He was raised by his grandmother. She taught him the language of the creatures in the forest and the voices of the woods. During his early years, Hiawatha roamed through the forests, talking with the animals, trees, and shrubs.

Then one day Hiawatha felt that he had reached the age when it was time to become a warrior. To test his strength, he followed a large deer into the forest and killed it with his bare hands. The deer's horns were his trophy. But Hiawatha was still not a warrior, for the strength of a warrior lies not only in his weapons. So

he went back into the forest and fasted for seven days and seven nights. He prayed to the Great Spirit for the strength to bring fellowship and goodwill to all mankind. The Great Spirit was moved by Hiawatha's concern for the peoples of the world. So he gave Hiawatha the knowledge to grow corn. The Indian hero returned to his village and taught his people how to grow this precious grain.

Hiawatha looked for other ways to help men prosper. He asked the birch tree to give him some bark so that he could "make a leaf so light that it would glide on the river's waters." The birch tree agreed, and gave Hiawatha the material with which to build a canoe. Then Hia-

watha called the men of his village together and showed them his new gift. And this, too he gave to mankind.

Hiawatha decided that it was time he took a wife. Against his grandmother's wishes, he chose beautiful Minnehaha. His grandmother was angry because Minnehaha did not come from their own tribe. "Choose a wife from your own people," warned the grandmother. But Hiawatha answered, "I wish peace to reign between my people, the Ojibwas, and Minnehaha's people, the Dakotas. Our marriage shall join the two tribes." So Hiawatha married Minnehaha and brought her to his village. A joyous celebration of peace was held.

The great Indian was contented, but he felt that his happiness would not last. Hiawatha knew that happiness, like all things, would soon vanish and that even its memory would be forgotten. So he decided to capture it for mankind. Hiawatha took some colors and on a piece of birch bark drew happiness. Hiawatha called it writing, and this gift, too, he gave to man. Through the years the brave Indian gave many gifts to his brothers and sisters. And they in turn gave them to others.

One day Hiawatha decided that it was time to leave the earth. He said a tearful farewell to his people and climbed into his birch canoe. The Indian hero sailed down the river until he reached the arms of the Great Spirit.

89

Walt Disney, creator of a wonderful world.

THE SLEEPING BEAUTY

A very long time ago there lived a king and a queen in a faraway land. They had a grand palace, great forests and gardens, and many faithful, loving subjects. Still, the king and queen were unhappy, for they had no children.

But one bright spring morning, there was great rejoicing in the palace. A beautiful daughter was born to the royal couple. The bells in the village church were rung, flags were unfurled, and invitations were sent to all parts of the kingdom bidding the people to come to the christening feast. Also invited to the feast were the six good fairies who lived in the kingdom. There was another fairy in the kingdom too, but she was an evil fairy, and she was the only one not asked to the celebration.

The day of the christening dawned with blue skies and a bright sun. The palace gates were thrown open and the people came bearing gifts of silver, gold, silks, and laces for the new princess.

At last the time came for the fairies to present their gifts to the little baby girl. One fairy stepped toward the cradle and said, "My gift to you is beauty." Another fairy added that the princess would become as kind and good as she was beautiful. The third, fourth, and fifth fairies offered the child the gifts of wisdom, love, song, and laughter.

Then, before anyone knew what had

91

happened, the evil fairy appeared from nowhere and stood before the cradle. She waved her wand and in a crackling voice said, "Even though you didn't invite me to the feast, I shall give the child a gift anyway. All my sisters' wishes shall indeed come true; but when the princess is 16 years old, she shall prick her finger on a spindle and die!" Then, with an evil laugh, the wicked fairy flew out of the garden. The king and queen were heartbroken and wept.

Just then the sixth fairy stepped forward. She said, "Fear not, for though I cannot undo my evil sister's wish, I can change it. The little princess shall not die,

but sleep—sleep until a king's son shall appear and awaken her with a kiss. And with the princess, the entire kingdom shall sleep until the prince breaks the spell with his kiss."

The grateful king raised his hand and everyone was silent. "My good people," he said, "I command that all spindles in the kingdom be burned." And indeed, all the spindles were hastily destroyed.

The years passed. They were happy ones for the princess, for each of the good fairies' wishes came true. She was the most beautiful princess in the world— kind and true, wise, loving, and cheerful.

On her 16th birthday the princess was given a celebration party. All of her friends were invited. But she soon tired of the dancing and games and went for a walk alone in the forest. There she discovered a lonely old tower. She climbed the winding staircase and, in a room at the very top of the tower, the princess found an old lady sitting at a spinning wheel. She asked if she might try the wheel herself. As the princess touched the spindle, she pricked her finger, and quickly fell asleep. The entire kingdom also fell into a deep slumber.

Nearly a hundred years passed. One day a handsome young prince from another kingdom happened upon an ancient

tower deep in the forest. The tower was covered with vines and branches. He pushed his way through the door and climbed the creaking staircase. At the top he came to the door of a small room. As the prince entered, he saw the beautiful sleeping princess. The prince gazed upon her, knelt, and kissed her. She stirred gently and awoke. Slowly all the people throughout the sleeping kingdom also awoke. Before long, life began again in the kingdom.

The king and queen were overjoyed. It was just as the fairies said it would be! But the happiest person in the kingdom was the prince, for he married the lovely Sleeping Beauty.

SNOW WHITE AND THE SEVEN DWARFS

At last! At last! Now we dwarfs can tell you all about our dear friend Snow White. And what a story it is!

"Let me . . . ho, ho, ho . . . tell it . . . ha, ha, ha, fellas!" shouted Happy. "Oh no, Happy, you'll laugh all the way through the story," replied Dopey.

"I think . . . ah-choo! . . . I ought to . . . ah-choo! . . . tell about Snow White," said Sneezy. "Never mind," answered the dwarfs, "you've wasted enough time already!"

"Grumpy will be the one," said Bashful. "He's got the best speaking voice."

"Okay, Grumpy," replied Doc, "we'll let you tell the girls and boys about Snow White."

And so, Grumpy began the story.

"Once upon a time, there was a queen who was expecting her first child. The queen, who was as good as she was beautiful, hoped that the baby would be a girl. And sure enough, one fine wintry morning, the queen gave birth to a splendid baby girl. She named the child Snow White. But, alas, a short time later, there was great sadness in the kingdom, for the good queen died.

Soon afterward the king married another wife. His new queen was beautiful and very proud. She could not bear to think that there was anyone in the entire kingdom as handsome as she. The new queen owned a magical mirror. She would spend hour upon hour gazing at her reflection in the looking glass and saying, "Mirror, mirror on the wall, who is the fairest of us all?" And, without fail, the mirror always answered, "Thou, queen, are fairest of them all."

Since the queen was so busy with her magic mirror, she paid very little attention to her stepdaughter. And it was no secret that Snow White had grown into a beautiful young girl. One day the queen asked her mirror the usual question. The looking glass replied, "Queen, you are full fair, 'tis true, but Snow White is fairer than you." When the queen heard this, she flew into a rage! She called to one of her servants and said, "Take Snow White into the forest and put her to death!"

Obeying the wicked queen's command, the servant took Snow White deep into the woods. But his heart melted when she begged him to spare her life. So the servant told her to flee, and never again to come near the castle.

Poor Snow White wandered alone through the forest. In the evening she came upon a tiny cottage. It was so small that she could barely squeeze through the door.

"That was our house," said Sleepy.

"Quiet," replied Grumpy, "let me finish the story."

"On the table were seven little bowls of soup. Famished after her long walk, Snow White gulped down all of the soup. Then she went upstairs to take a short nap.

"This is where we come in," said Happy, happily. Grumpy paid no attention and continued with his story.

"We seven dwarfs came marching into the cottage. Imagine the surprise on our faces when we discovered that all the soup had been eaten and a beautiful stranger was asleep in our beds! Sneezy was so excited that he let out one of his

mightiest sneezes. Happy laughed like mad, and Sleepy did something most unusual—he somehow managed to stay wide awake.

Snow White awoke with a start. After we introduced ourselves, she told us all about her stepmother and the magical mirror. We took pity on poor Snow White and invited her to stay with us.

Meanwhile, back at the palace, the queen gazed into her mirror and again asked the looking glass the same old question. The mirror replied, "Queen, thou are of beauty rare, but Snow White, living in the glen with seven little men, is a thousand times more fair."

Furious because she had been tricked, the queen thought up different ways to do away with Snow White. Twice she disguised herself as an old woman and journeyed to the dwarfs' cottage to get rid of her stepdaughter. But both times

the dwarfs returned just in time to save their guest from certain death.

After the second attempt, the queen went into her chamber in the castle and prepared a poisoned apple. The outside of the fruit was very rosy and tempting, but whoever tasted it was sure to die. This would do the trick, thought the queen. She dressed as an old peasant woman and

once again made her way back to the dwarfs' cottage.

When she reached the door, she knocked and shouted, "Apples, fresh apples, apples for sale." Snow White rushed to answer the door. The old queen offered her a piece of fruit, and, without thinking, Snow White took the bright red apple and bit into it. She had scarcely put the piece of apple into her mouth when she fell dead upon the ground. The queen laughed with glee and rushed back to her castle.

That evening, when we dwarfs returned to the cottage, we found poor Snow White. Heartbroken, Dopey put the beautiful princess in a coffin of glass and placed the coffin high on a hilltop. There she could be kissed by the sun, moon, and stars.

Then one day—you guessed it—a handsome prince happened by. He came upon Snow White, and even though she was

dead, he found her beauty so rare that he fell in love with her. The prince decided to carry the coffin back to his palace. But the moment he lifted it, the piece of apple fell from Snow White's lips. She stirred and all of a sudden came to life again—even more beautiful than before.

Naturally the grateful Snow White married the prince, for she truly loved him. The wicked queen, on hearing the news of the marriage, went into a rage, broke her mirror, and suddenly fell dead. Need we say that everyone else in the story lived happily ever after?"

CINDERELLA

Once upon a time the wife of a very rich man took ill, and feeling that she was about to die, called her only daughter, a young girl, to her bedside. She made the girl promise always to be good. In exchange for her promise, she would be protected by heaven. The daughter promised and the mother died happily.

Some years later the young girl's father married a widow who had two daughters. The stepmother and stepsisters treated the young girl terribly from the very start. They kept her busy washing pots and pans, doing the laundry, and

cleaning the entire house. After a hard day's work she would sometimes rest near the cinders and ashes in the fireplace, so she came to be called Cinderella.

But Cinderella remembered her promise to her mother and she was as good and as kind as her stepsisters were bad. Because she was not allowed to leave the house and make friends, she took care of all the animals in the neighborhood. Birds, horses, cats and dogs, and even lizards, snails, and mice were her friends. The

birds kept her company with their songs while she worked. So, although Cinderella was treated cruelly by her stepmother and stepsisters, her days were spent happily in the company of her animal friends.

Now it happened that the king decided to give a ball for his son and he invited all the young women in the kingdom. Cinderella asked her stepmother whether she too might go to the ball. But her stepmother just laughed. "You at the king's ball?," she snickered. "Why you're covered with cinders and ashes and you haven't even got a ball gown to wear. Now help us get dressed, you lazy thing, and don't be silly!"

But Cinderella had a plan. She had kept all the scraps of material left over from her stepsisters' gowns, and since she was an excellent seamstress, before you could say "Boo" she had made herself a beautiful gown. When her stepsisters saw how lovely she looked, their envy knew no bounds. They ripped the gown off her back and accused her of having stolen the material.

So, smug and satisfied as only wicked people can be after they've mistreated someone, the stepmother and her daughters set off triumphantly for the ball. Cinderella, left behind, began to sob her poor heart out, when all of a sudden she felt somebody touch her shoulder. She turned and saw an old woman smiling at her. "Who are you?" asked Cinderella. "I am your fairy godmother," replied the old woman.

Then, wasting no time, the old woman waved her magic wand and the surprised Cinderella found herself dressed in the most magnificent ball gown she had ever

seen. A few more waves of the wand and Cinderella's tiny animal friends were turned into a coachman, footmen, and six white horses. Another wave of the wand and a large yellow pumpkin became a coach.

"Now go to the ball," said the fairy godmother. "But remember, you must be back by midnight—for at that hour the spell will be broken."

Cinderella promised not to forget. She thanked the good fairy and set out for the royal palace. When she got there, no one recognized her, but all admired her— especially the prince, who danced with her the whole evening.

So happy was Cinderella that she forgot to watch the time, and only remembered when the tower clock began to strike twelve. "Oh, my," she thought and fled, losing one of her glass slippers. She was just able to get out of the prince's sight when the clock struck midnight. The coach immediately turned back into a pumpkin, the footmen became mice again, and her beautiful gown was once more a cinder-covered, ragged dress.

All the prince had left was a tiny glass slipper. But he realized that he loved the young woman who had worn it. He sent off a messenger to find its owner, announcing that he would marry the woman who could fit the slipper. The messenger searched throughout the kingdom but could find no one whose foot fit the tiny shoe. Finally he came to Cinderella's house.

The stepsisters were very excited. They tried and tried to fit into the tiny slipper, but their feet were much too big. The messenger asked if there were any other young women in the house. "There's only Cinderella," answered her father. "Cinderella?" said the stepmother. "That dirty, lazy thing? How can you even mention her." But the messenger, who was losing hope, asked to see Cinderella, dirty though she might be.

Cinderella came forward shyly. The glass slipper was tried on, and of course it fit. She was then taken to the royal palace where a great wedding celebration was held, and the prince and Cinderella lived happily ever after.

The stepsisters almost died with envy, but Cinderella, good as she was, brought them to live at the palace and even found suitable husbands for each of them to marry.

THE UGLY DUCKLING

The whole forest was excited, but Mamma Duck especially could hardly sit still, for it was a very special time.

"What's the matter?" asked a passing bluejay.

"The eggs are about to hatch. In just a few minutes I'll have seven little ducklings to take care of!"

"Good luck!" said the jay and he flew off.

And, in fact, in just a short while the seven eggs hatched, one by one, to Mamma Duck's great happiness. In no time at all the forest was filled with the noisy quack-quack of seven hungry little ducks. Mamma Duck took the commotion calmly. She smoothed their feathers and got them all in line and then marched proudly at the head of the parade to show off her new family to her friends. They hadn't gotten very far when. . . .

"Coooo, why is your last little one so ugly?" asked an old hen.

"Ugly? My child . . . ugly?" stammered Mamma Duck, looking at her family more closely. Having done so, she saw that the duckling at the end of the line did not look quite right. In fact, he did not even look like a duckling at all.

"Why, you *are* ugly!" she exclaimed. "I'm sure that the egg that hatched you must have rolled into my nest by mistake. You're certainly not my child. Now go away before I snap at you."

And things being as they were, all the poor little duckling could do was to set out to try to find his real mother, though he had no idea who she might be. He walked and he walked until finally he came to a large farm.

"Oh, kind lady, are you my mother?" he asked a turkey.

"How dare you? Are you making fun?" replied the turkey. "Why, I never had such an ugly child. Go away!"

"Dear madam, have you lost a child?" asked the poor duckling, turning to a fat hen who was busy caring for her brood of little yellow chicks.

"Just listen to what this fellow is asking!" she shouted to her husband, the rooster. The rooster didn't even bother to answer. He just flew straight at the ugly duckling to teach him a lesson, which he proceeded to do with a few well-aimed pecks of his sharp beak.

The little duckling, his heart broken, left the farm and set off slowly down a path that led to some woods. Along the way he met a brown pheasant leading her band of fat little baby pheasants, all of whom looked just like her.

"Oh, how beautiful you are! Perhaps you are my mother?" asked the little duckling hopefully.

"But, my dear boy! Have you ever

looked at yourself in the mirror?" laughed the mother pheasant.

So the poor, tired, hungry little duckling continued his wandering. Reaching a lake, he chanced to gaze into the calm, mirror-like waters . . . and saw his own reflection.

"Oh, how ugly I am," he cried.

"You are not ugly at all," announced a voice nearby. "And I've finally found you, my child!" The duckling looked around and, wonder of wonders, he saw a beautiful swan surrounded by many other little "ducklings" who all looked the same as he.

"Others may call you ugly, but to me you are the most beautiful child in the world, and when you grow up, you'll be a beautiful swan."

And that is just what happened.

PUSS IN BOOTS

Once upon a time in a faraway land where strange things often happen that almost never seem to happen here, a very poor young man was sitting sadly, alone except for a large cat. The young man was sad because his beloved father had just died. He was poor because his father had left only debts—and a cat.

There is nothing else to be done, he thought. My father wished it so, and so it must be. And the sad young man looked fondly down at the cat that his father had left in his care on his deathbed. The cat purred softly.

"My poor cat! It is not that I don't like you. But I have so many debts that I can hardly feed myself. Where will I find the money to care for you?" wondered the young man. And he leaned over to pat the cat absentmindedly.

"If that is all that is bothering you, master, do not give it a second thought," said the cat to the young man's great amazement, for he had never heard of a talking cat.

"Just buy me a pair of boots, and I promise you that we'll go a long way with them. Indeed, I will make you rich and famous!"

With some hesitation the young man agreed, and provided the cat with the boots he had asked for.

When the cat had slipped the boots on, he took up a large pack and headed straight for the woods. He stopped under a tree, lay down, and pretended to sleep.

Soon a large hare came up and sniffed the pack to see if it contained anything good to eat. Quick as a flash the cat slipped the hare into the pack. He hoisted it onto his shoulders and headed off to the court of the king.

"Good day, Your Majesty. My master, the Marquis of Carabas, sent me with this gift."

"Why thank you," said the king. "How very kind of the Marquis."

The next day the cat brought a plump pheasant to the king, having gotten it the same way as he did the hare. And the day after there was another gift for the king. Finally, the king wished to see this generous Marquis of Carabas and sent the cat to invite him to the court.

Quick as a wink the cat ran to his master and suggested that he bathe in the river. The young man made no objection, for by now he trusted the faithful cat completely. While the young man was swimming, the cat took away his ragged clothes, for he knew that the king and all his court would soon be passing.

"Help! Help!" cried the cat. "My master, the Marquis of Carabas, is drowning." Quickly one of the king's courtiers threw the young man a rope and pulled

119

home of a terrifying ogre who could change himself into the shape of any animal. The cat, using all his cunning, had asked the ogre to transform himself first into a lion and then into a mouse. And, being a cat, he ate up the mouse-ogre in one quick bite. And that is how the young man found himself master of the castle and all the vast lands that had belonged to the ogre.

Of course, when the king saw all this he decided that the young man would be an excellent match for his daughter. And it wasn't hard to convince the young man.

So Puss in Boots kept his promise.

him to the riverbank. Just then the cat yelled: "Help! Help! Someone has stolen my master's clothes." The king then ordered a messenger to run to the palace and bring the "marquis" an elegant suit of clothes worthy of his rank.

Beautifully dressed, the young man hardly recognized himself. But he played along as the cat solemnly presented him to the king, who invited him to accompany him on a ride through the countryside. As the "marquis" climbed into the royal carriage, he found himself seated next to a beautiful princess.

"It might be a good idea to look out over your lands, master," suggested the cat. The young man's eyes opened wide at this, for he didn't have any lands. And they opened wider still when, leaning out of the carriage window, he saw the peasants in the fields all tip their hats to him as he went by. But the cat had been busy. Before the carriage arrived, he had told the peasants that the king was coming, so naturally when the carriage passed by they all courteously tipped their hats.

Finally the king's carriage arrived at an immense castle whose hundreds of towers stretched high into the sky. This was the

LITTLE RED RIDING HOOD

Once upon a time there lived a little girl who was so good that everyone loved her, especially her grandmother, who gave her all sorts of wonderful presents. One of these was a red wool cape. She liked it so much she wore it all the time, and so everyone called her Little Red Riding Hood. One day her mother said, "Little Red Riding Hood, take this food over to grandmother's. She is not feeling well. But remember to follow the path and don't stray off into the woods."

The little girl had only gone a short way when she met a wolf. Since she was a polite girl, she said, "Good afternoon, Mr. Wolf." "Good afternoon to you, Little Red Riding Hood," replied the wolf. "Where are you going?"

When Little Red Riding Hood told him, the wolf thought, "This little girl will make a juicy meal, but if I'm smart I can eat her and her grandmother too." Thinking quickly, the wily wolf said, "See those beautiful flowers? Why not pick some and take them to your grandmother?" "Grandma would like that," said Little Red Riding Hood. She thanked the wolf, and left the path to pick some flowers in the woods. While she was doing this, the wolf hurried to grandmother's house and knocked on her door.

"Who is it?" asked grandmother. "It's Little Red Red Riding Hood," replied the wolf in a high voice. "Well, come in, dear," said grandmother. The wolf didn't wait for her to invite him twice. In one leap he jumped onto the bed and swallowed the old lady in a single gulp. Then he put on her clothes and cap and pulled the covers up to his long nose.

Meanwhile, Little Red Riding Hood arrived at the house with the flowers. "Hello Grandma," she said, but for some reason she was very afraid. "Oh, Grandma! what big ears you have!" exclaimed Little Red Riding Hood. "The better to hear you with, my dear," croaked the wolf. "Oh, Grandma! What big hands you have!" said the little girl in a frightened voice. "The better to catch you with, my dear.

"And, Grandma, what a big mouth you have!" said the little girl in a frightened voice. "The better to eat you with,

my dear!" shouted the wolf. And he bounded out of bed and swallowed her in a single bite.

Stuffed from his double lunch, the wolf fell into a deep sleep. His snoring was so loud that it could be heard for miles around. In fact a hunter passing by and hearing the loud snores thought to himself, "Listen to the old lady snore. Maybe I'd better go and have a look. She may be ill."

He entered the cottage and, approaching the bed, saw to his surprise the sleeping wolf. He raised his gun to shoot him, but then he remembered the grandmother and guessed that the wolf had eaten her. So he took a sharp knife and cut the wolf open. Out jumped Little Red Riding Hood. "Oh, what a fright I've had!" she said. "How black it was inside the wolf's belly." In no time at all Little Red Riding Hood's grandmother was freed too, and just in time.

When both were safe, the hunter took some large stones and placed them in the hole left in the belly of the wolf. He then sewed up the hole and all three hid to wait for the wolf to awaken.

When the wolf finally woke up, he knew that something wasn't quite right. He had had a huge meal, but he was still hungry. At the same time, he felt unusually full. He decided to take to his heels. The others laughed as he tried to run weighted down with the heavy stones. In a few steps the hunter caught up with him and shot him.

The hunter was happy because he had finally caught the wolf. Grandma was happy because, thanks to the food and flowers, she now felt much better. And, last but not least, Little Red Riding Hood was glad because her scary adventure had taught her a lesson. In fact she solemnly promised her mother never to disobey her again.

INDEX

A

Aesop, Greek fabulist, 9
Aladdin and His Wonderful Lamp, 24–26
Ali Baba and the Forty Thieves, 19–23
Andersen, Hans Christian, Danish author, 9, 65

B

Banker and the Cobbler, The, 35
Bashful, one of the seven dwarfs, 99
Blue Beard, 41–42
Bremen Town Musicians, The 57–59

C

Cinderella, 109–15
Crow and the Jug, The, 16

D

Doc, one of the seven dwarfs, 99
Dopey, one of the seven dwarfs, 99, 105

E

Eleven Wild Swans, The, 76–78
Emperor's New Clothes, The, 70–72
Enkidú, friend of Gilgamesh, 10

F

Fables, 9
Banker and the Cobbler, The, 35
Crow and the Jug, The, 16
Lion and the Mouse, The, 15–16
Mosquito and the Bull, The, 17
Peasant and his Sons, The, 33
Wolf and the Stork, The, 34
Fairy Tales, 9
Aladdin and His Wonderful Lamp, 24–26
Ali Baba and the Forty Thieves, 19–23
Blue Beard, 41
Bremen Town Musicians, The, 57–59
Cinderella, 109–15
Eleven Wild Swans, The, 76–78

Emperor's New Clothes, The, 70–72
Genie of the River, The, 29–31
Hansel and Gretel, 45–48
King of the Golden Mountain, The, 60–61
Little Match Girl, The, 73–75
Little Mermaid, The, 65–68
Little Red Riding Hood, 121–22
Little Tin Soldier, The, 82–83
Magic Table, The, 54–56
Princess and the Pea, The, 79–81
Princess Briar Rose, 43
Puss in Boots, 118–20
Rapunzel, 51–53
Red Shoes, The, 68–69
Seven Ravens, The, 49–50
Shoemaker and the Elves, The, 61–62
Sleeping Beauty, The, 91–94
Snow White and the Seven Dwarfs, 99–107
Tinder Box, The, 84–85
Tom Thumb, 37–40
Ugly Duckling, The, 116–117

G

Genie of the River, The, 29–31
Ghiase, fairy tale hero, 29, 30, 31
Gilgamesh, The Adventures of, 9–12
Grimm, Jacob and Wilhelm, German fairy tale writers, 9, 45
Grumpy, one of the seven dwarfs, 99, 103

H

Hansel and Gretel, 45–48
Happy, one of the seven dwarfs, 99, 103, 104
Hiawatha, The Song of, 86–87

K

Kassim, brother of Ali Baba, 19, 22
King of the Golden Mountain, The, 60–61

L

La Fontaine, Jean de, French fabulist, 9, 33
Legends
Gilgamesh, The Adventures of, 9–12
Hiawatha, The Song of, 86–87
Lion and the Mouse, The, 15–16

Little Match Girl, The, 73–75
Little Mermaid, The, 65–68
Little Red Riding Hood, 121–22
Little Tin Soldier, The, 82–83

M

Magic Table, The, 54–56
Merlin, magician, 37
Minnehaha, legendary Indian princess, 87
Moon Flower, Alladin's wife, 24, 25, 26
Morgiana, Ali Baba's slave girl, 22, 23
Mosquito and the Bull, The, 17

N

Nemorina, fairy, 38, 40

O

"Open Seseme," command, 19–20

P

Peasant and his Sons, The, 33
Perrault, Charles, French writer, 9, 37
Phaedrus, Roman fabulist, 9
Princess and the Pea, The, 79–81
Princess Briar Rose, 43
Puss in Boots, 118–20

R

Rapunzel, 51–53
Red Shoes, The, 68–69
Rose Red, Blue Beard's wife, 41

S

Sambu, fairy tale heroine, 29, 30, 31
Seven dwarfs, the, 99–107
Seven Ravens, The, 49–50
Shoemaker and the Elves, The, 61–62
Sleeping Beauty, The, 91–94
Sleepy, one of the seven dwarfs, 103, 104
Sneezy, one of the seven dwarfs, 99, 103
Snow White and the Seven Dwarfs, 99–107
Song of Hiawatha, The, 86–87

T

Tinder Box, The, 84–85
Tom Thumb, 37–40

U

Ugly Duckling, The, 116–17
Ut-napishtim, ancient ancestor of Gilgamesh, 10, 12

W

Wolf and the Stork, The, 34